HARPER
AND THE
Night Forest

For Amelie, the queen of fairy tales and for the wild ones
who dream of enchanted forests . . . xxx
C.B.

Text copyright © Cerrie Burnell, 2017
Illustrations copyright © Laura Ellen Anderson, 2017

First published in the United Kingdom by Scholastic Children's Books, an
imprint of Scholastic Ltd, 2017.

This hardcover edition published by Sky Pony Press, 2018.

This is a work of fiction. Names, characters, places, and incidents are from
the author's imagination and used fictitiously.

Sky Pony Press books may be purchased in bulk at special discounts for
sales promotion, corporate gifts, fund-raising, or educational purposes. Special
editions can also be created to specifications. For details, contact the Special
Sales Department, Sky Pony Press, 307 West 36th Street, 11th Floor, New
York, NY 10018 or info@skyhorsepublishing.com.

Sky Pony® is a registered trademark of Skyhorse Publishing, Inc.®,
a Delaware corporation.

Visit our website at www.skyponypress.com

10 9 8 7 6 5 4 3 2 1

Library of Congress Cataloging-in-Publication Data available on file.

Jacket illustration © Laura Ellen Anderson
Jacket design by Kate Gartner

Hardcover ISBN: 978-1-5107-3483-8
EBook ISBN: 978-1-5107-3485-2

Printed in the United States of America

HARPER
AND THE
Night Forest

CERRIE BURNELL

Illustrated by Laura Ellen Anderson

Sky Pony Press
New York

Once there was a girl called Harper who had a rare musical gift. She heard songs on the wind, rhythms on the rain, and hope in the beat of a butterfly's wing. Harper could play every instrument she ever picked up, without learning a single note, but her favorite of all was her harp. Yet sometimes late at night, alone with her cat, Midnight, Harper imagined an instrument that made her heart soar. An instrument stitched from silver-lined cloud that drifted through all of her dreams . . .

Chapter One
THE LEATHER-BOUND BOOK

Star-stealer cloud swept through the sky and rain as steady as the beat of your heart drummed across the City of Clouds. On the fourteenth floor of the Tall Apartment Block, Harper crept out of her little flat, opened her Scarlet Umbrella, and floated down the stairs, lightly as a

3

feather. Three paces behind her prowled Midnight, her most unusual cat. He'd been named after the hour he had turned up at Harper's home, and she never went anywhere without him.

As they reached the tenth floor, the little cat paused and the umbrella swirled to stillness, hanging in the air like the bud of dandelion. Harper clutched the umbrella's silver handle with one hand and pulled her piccolo flute from her pocket with the other, then played a little ditty that echoed down the stairwells.

Beside her, an indigo door opened, and out stepped a boy who moved as quietly as a whisper: Nate Nathanielson.

"I need your help," said Harper brightly.

Nate nodded and gave a soft, low whistle; there was a swish of silvery fur and a wolf of mist-like majesty padded

out of the door, giving Harper's rain boot a friendly lick.

"Hello, Smoke." Harper giggled, tickling the wolf's ears before they set off down the stairs, Harper drifting in front and the others trailing behind.

On the fifth floor, Harper stopped to play a longer tune, and Nate joined in on his tambourine, while Midnight pranced and Smoke howled. Two rowdy children came tumbling out of the messy little flat.

"Liesel," said Harper, smiling as she hugged a small girl with filthy fingernails and a pink dove nesting in her tangled hair.

"Ferdie." Nate grinned, helping a boy with a serious scarf and serious frown to his feet.

"Come with me," called Harper, and they set off down the stairs and into the Unforgotten Concert Hall in the basement of their home.

Once inside, the children rushed across the stage, through the Forbidden Door, and into the Library of Long-Forgotten Music, a place that was full of dusty magic and the scent of secret songs.

"It's Great Aunt Sassy's birthday soon," Harper explained as they gazed around.

"I want to find a piece of harp music to play that's never been heard before."

Ferdie gave a serious nod. "Something mysterious and marvelous," he murmured.

"Something long forgotten," added Nate.

"Something very secret," hissed Liesel, scuttling away like a mouse.

Ferdie set off for the other side of the library with a long-legged stride. Nate and Smoke vanished into the darkest part of the room, moving through the shadows as if they were daylight. "If you find anything, play three sharp notes," called Harper. "Music is our secret signal."

You see, wherever the children went, they always carried their instruments.

Liesel had a shiny violin strapped to her back, Ferdie carried a button accordion, and Nate had his trusty tambourine on his pork-pie cap. As for Harper, her pockets were bursting with maracas and recorders and her beloved harp, all of which she could play.

Harper and Midnight wandered through the dusty air, searching through long-lost music books. They opened one called *Nightingale's Sorrow*, leafed through another called *Midnight Dreamers*, and glanced at a blue leather-bound book with no name, just a magnificent songbird etched upon the cover. They climbed up high and crawled down low, but nothing quite seemed right. Then a cobweb caught on one of Midnight's whiskers and he gave a sudden sneeze, knocking over a whole shelf of sheet music.

Liesel shot out of the gloominess and caught the falling pages. "Thanks," said Harper, ruffling the small girl's hair and awakening Storm, the pink dove. Storm was actually Harper's pet, a gift from her parents who were traveling the world in a floating circus, but Liesel's knotted locks made the perfect little nest.

"I think Ferdie's found something." Liesel grinned.

Ferdie came strolling over, clutching an

armful of books. "I found a trombone solo, a song for the melodeon, and some amazing tunes for the piano, but nothing yet for a harp. . . . Maybe Nate's had more luck?"

The three children peered across the library at the boy with the wolf. Nate, who only saw lightness or darkness, was running his fingers over each forgotton songbook, feeling the papery thinness of them. He could always tell how old a book was by the creases that crossed its pages, and these books were very old indeed.

Beside him, Smoke gave an intelligent growl and pulled at a book with her teeth. The children hurried over and Harper carefully took the book from the wolf's silvery jaws. It was the very same leather-bound book she had glanced at earlier. Its cover was a pale, faded blue, with the magnificent songbird etched in gold.

"It looks like a book of spells," whispered Ferdie.

"Open it," snapped Liesel, hopping wildly with excitement.

The book seemed to shuffle itself to page seven in Harper's hands. "That's incredible." She gasped. "It's a harp solo called 'Night Flight.'"

Harper's three friends looked amazed.

"It sounds perfect," said Ferdie.

"Play it now," begged Liesel.

"We'll join in the chorus," offered Nate.

Harper raised her small golden harp into the air, but before she had a chance to pluck a single string, Midnight's tail flicked, Smoke's fur rose along her back, and Storm gave a warning cry. Someone else was in the library.

The children huddled close together as a shadow swept through the crowded bookcases.

"Who could be down here?" whispered Nate in a voice as quiet as snow.

"No one else knows this library exists," Ferdie mumbled.

"No one . . ." began Harper, but her voice trailed off. Midnight leaped into her arms and Smoke gave a strange growl as from within the dust emerged a man with magpie-feather hair. "No one except the Wild Conductor!" Harper exclaimed.

"Greetings," said the terrifyingly tall man, sinking into a low, elegant bow.

"Oh, it's you," said Liesel with a bored look.

The Wild Conductor gave a half smile. He didn't care much for children. But Harper's musical gift had astonished him so much that he had become very fond of her and her friends.

"What are you doing down here anyway?" Liesel went on.

The Wild Conductor stooped down low as if he were letting the children in on a highly important secret. "Searching for an extraordinary music book." He sighed. "A book that holds the one song that can draw an Ice Raven out of the trees."

Ferdie at once began imagining a poem called "Bird of Ice and Feathers." Nate began wondering what sort of enchanting forest an Ice Raven might live in.

Liesel tried to picture the mystical bird, but all she could think of was a magnificent songbird etched in gold. "What does this music book look like?" she asked cautiously.

The Wild Conductor rose to his full height. "Very old, very odd, very special. It has no name, just a sketch of the Ice Raven on its cover."

The children fidgeted uncomfortably. "Like this?" asked Harper quietly as she held up the beautiful leather-bound book.

The Wild Conductor's eyes shimmered

dangerously, and for a moment, he seemed to go into a trance. "Yes!" he half spat. "Give it to me!" And with a swirl of his black satin coat, he snatched the book from Harper's grasp.

Chapter Two
THE WILD CONDUCTOR'S DREAM

In a heartbeat, the children sprang into action. For if there was one thing they were used to dealing with, it was the tricks of the Wild Conductor. Liesel clambered up the side of bookcase and reached out to grab the tall man's hat. Ferdie stuck out a foot to trip him. Nate whispered to Smoke and the wolf got ready to pounce. Midnight leaped onto the tall man's shoulders, digging in his claws, while Storm flew in a ring around the library, screaming a war cry.

But Harper didn't move. Instead, she stared at the Wild Conductor and said, "Listen. We found that book, and if you don't tell us why you need it, we'll take it right back," and she lifted the book firmly from his hands.

The Wild Conductor was startled into an apology. "I do beg your pardon," he muttered darkly. "It's just that I am creating an orchestra of ravens to win back my place in the Circus of Dreams."

The children nodded solemnly and

at once began to whisper. They had all visited the Circus of Dreams and knew of its strange and glorious wonders.

"Legend has it that in the Night Forest there lives an Ice Raven whose song can tame the fiercest heart," the Wild Conductor continued. "If I had that mythical bird in my orchestra, I could tame Othello Grande's heart and rejoin the circus."

Harper was still as she thought of Othello Grande, the fearful ringmaster of the Circus of Dreams who let few join his circus and even fewer leave. She remembered how the Wild Conductor had helped her draw that very circus across the sky so she could be reunited with her parents, who lived in its floating tents. Slowly, Harper held out the book. "In that case, it's yours." She smiled.

The Wild Conductor was pale with shock. He wasn't used to people being so kind. "Th-thank you," he stuttered, his voice dipping very low.

"There's just one thing you need to do, though," said Harper, a glint of excitement twinkling in her eyes. "You have to take us with you!"

The wonderful Wild Conductor gave a rare and slightly shocking laugh. "It would be my greatest honor," he said with a nod.

"You mean we're going to the Night Forest?" asked Ferdie.

"Near the City of Singing Clocks?" murmured Nate.

"Where fairy tales first began," squealed Liesel, who had a love of black trees and wicked-hearted witches.

The Wild Conductor nodded. Suddenly, the library of Long-Forgotten Music was filled with the sound of cheering and howling and a thousand happy meows.

Up the creaky staircase they all charged, back to the Tall Apartment Block. On the fifth floor, everyone paused for breath as Ferdie and Liesel crashed into a little flat so crowded with stories it could have been a bookstore. "Mama, Papa, can we go to the Night Forest with the Wild

Conductor to find an Ice Raven?" Liesel screamed, her small heart racing.

Their father, Peter, a famous German writer, leaned out of his messy study and gave a surprised frown. "You mean the one near the City of Singing Clocks?" he exclaimed.

"Yes!" yelled Ferdie, tightening his serious scarf.

Brigitte, their mother, looked up from fixing Ferdie's kite and chuckled. "Well, actually, maybe you can. Your father is launching his new book there next week. I think we could all join him for a vacation."

Ferdie punched the air and Liesel

pirouetted almost as high as the fluttering pink dove. The Wild Conductor gave a small nod of gratitude and then followed the children to the tenth floor.

Everyone sat waiting on the stairs in near silence, the soft, panting breath of the wolf echoing their quivering hearts. What would Nate's mom say?

"Hello, Narla," said the Wild Conductor as Nate's beautiful mother leaned out of her indigo doorway. Narla raised her eyebrows curiously as they made their request.

Harper pushed her hands into her pockets, crossing her fingers for luck. Then the wolf did something wonderful. She rose onto her mist-colored paws and padded over to the Wild Conductor, settling obediently at his feet.

Narla smiled. "Well, if Smoke thinks it's a good idea, then I suppose I can't say no." Everyone heaved a sigh of relief and Nate buried his face in Smoke's dusky fur. She really was quite an astounding creature.

Harper left her rejoicing friends and skipped up the stairs to the little flat she lived in with her Great Aunt Sassy. Midnight prowled three paces behind and Storm fluttered brightly ahead.

Inside their little flat, Great Aunt Sassy was hard at work making costumes for the Dutch Opera House. "Ferdie and Liesel's family is going to the Night Forest with Nate and the Wild Conductor," said Harper breathlessly. "There will be black trees and singing clocks and an Ice Raven who can tame the fiercest heart."

Sassy put down the green felt hat she was decorating and swept Harper into a lavender-scented hug. "Well, my darling, I could hardly stand in the way of such a grand adventure. Of course you must go!"

"Thank you," murmured Harper, and as Summer-dew rain beat a gentle lullaby against the windows, stars awoke across the City of Clouds. Harper snuggled down to sleep—to dream of deep, dark woods and mysterious clouds that rained music as sweet as a nightingale's song.

Chapter Three
THE BICYCLE AND THE RAVENS

The very next morning, Harper stood on the rooftop of the Tall Apartment Block, gazing across the City of Clouds. The pale light of morning turned the puddles sunrise-blue, so the city looked like a lake made of dawn. As she stared at the streets she so loved, the dream she kept having drifted back to her. It was always the same: Harper was playing a storm cloud as if it were an accordion, but instead of rain, it spilled notes of music. "If only it were real." She sighed.

The whirr of propeller blades came spinning through the air, chasing all thoughts of Harper's dream away. The Dutch Opera House helicopter had arrived to take everyone to the City of Singing Clocks. The German family and Great Aunt Sassy would travel in their helicopter. Harper and Nate were to be towed behind in the Scarlet Umbrella.

"How is the Wild Conductor going to get there?" asked Harper, helping her friends load their suitcases.

"I'm not really sure," said Peter, scratching his head.

"Don't forget, he was once a world-famous magician," said Brigitte. "I'm sure he'll come up with something."

Ferdie gave Harper a serious salute and Liesel did a quick-footed curtsy. "See you in the City of Singing Clocks," they said, laughing.

Harper waved and hurried over to Nate, who was busily attaching the Scarlet Umbrella to the helicopter's hovering tail with edentwine, an unbreakable string woven from storm-bloom stems. Nate gave the twine three sharp tugs to make certain it was secure, and then Harper flung open the umbrella, spun it upside down, and leaped in, Midnight bounding at her heels.

Nate climbed carefully in after her, whistling for Smoke. With a wild, graceful pounce that nearly took Harper's breath away, the wolf joined them in the umbrella.

"Farewell, Tall Apartment Block," Harper murmured, and then the helicopter took to the skies and they were whisked sharply up through cascades of raindrops and Feather-fern clouds, with a rush of air that made the wolf howl.

Flying by umbrella is always an adventure. It's a feeling of being lighter than dandelions, as if you were made entirely from cloud. It was something that both Harper and Nate were used to, and yet it never lost its wonder. But as the helicopter lurched through the sky, the world became a blur of fog and air.

"Hold on," cried Nate, gripping the scarlet fabric with one hand and throwing the other arm around Smoke.

Harper ducked down deeper, seizing the umbrella's handle and clutching Midnight close. "It's like being pulled through the sky by a speedboat." She chuckled as they bumped through sunlight and rain. Then, beyond the trill of the propeller, came the powerful beat of shadowy wings. Harper peeked over the edge of the umbrella and felt her mouth fall open so widely she almost swallowed a patch of rainbow.

She grabbed Nate's hand so that he knew something terrifying or something extraordinary was about to happen. He leaned in close. "What can you see?"

Inside the helicopter, Ferdie and Liesel peered out the open window. They had never been quite this high before, or flown this fast. The helicopter felt wiggly and wild, as if they were tumbling through the air in a craft made of thunder. It was a lot more exciting than Liesel had imagined, even if it meant she couldn't travel by umbrella with her friends.

Ferdie was loving every moment. He

reached for the pencil that was tucked behind his ear, excited to scribble down his many poetic thoughts, but his hand froze halfway to the page. "Look!" he yelled, pointing at something far off in the clouds as a feeling of awe swept over him.

Liesel sat still, her eyes glittering with glee. For peddling through the sky on a bicycle held afloat by a chorus of dark birds came the Wild Conductor, his dark satin coat swirling like a cape of night sky.

The birds looked like doves cut from darkness. "Their feathers are the same shade as the Wild Conductor's hair," Harper whispered.

Nate could just make out the shape of a man cycling through the air, a cloud of great wings surrounding him. It was a very odd sight indeed.

The funniest thing about it was the birds themselves, for though they were proud and fierce, they squabbled like a pack of grumpy turkeys. A furious wind shrieked a shrill whistle and two of the biggest ravens started attacking each other. Beak by beak, every bird was pulled into a mid-air scuffle. The edentwine that bound them became dangerously tangled and the bicycle began twirling out of control.

"The Wild Conductor's in trouble," gasped Harper. "The ravens aren't used

40

to flying in such strong wind."

Midnight scrabbled into the depths of the umbrella's scarlet dome and tugged a small harp onto Harper's lap. Nate could make out the harp's golden gleam and he at once understood what the cat was trying to do. "Remember the time you got every bird in the central aviary to follow your music?" Nate bellowed. "See if you can do it again."

Slowly, Harper stood up. Smoke curled her soft body around Harper's legs so she couldn't wobble, while Midnight climbed onto Harper's head, keeping her warm in the wind. Harper raised the golden harp into the air and waited for the notes to come to her. Then her fingers were

moving of their own accord, playing a melody of dark feathers and brave flight, a song so wonderful that even the whistling wind picked up her tune and calmed the clouds.

Storm, the little dove who had been sleeping in Harper's pocket, awoke and soared into the air, her clear cry in harmony with the harp. The ravens eyed her angrily, but instead of swooping at her, they began to follow her until, at last, their wings beat in time and they moved through the sky like a great black balloon.

The Wild Conductor tipped his hat to

Harper, his eyes filled with the deepest respect. He watched the way his birds obeyed her every note and a dark smile spread across his face. "She is perfect for capturing an Ice Raven," he muttered. Then he looked down and gave a delighted cough, for below them lay a city that was home to a thousand singing clocks.

Chapter Four
THE CITY OF SINGING CLOCKS

Harper caught her breath as a fairy-tale city came into view on the edge of a looming forest. "What's it like?" asked Nate, who could sense the black mass of land where the trees began.

"Everything looks thousands of years old," squealed Liesel from the helicopter.

"There are steeples and turrets and towers of twisting staircases," added Ferdie, already imagining the opening sentence of his fabulous first book.

"There's a fantastical castle and a river that's far too blue," said the Wild Conductor coolly, yet even he couldn't help but be spellbound.

The main clock in the market square struck twelve and a hundred happy cuckoos burst from their painted wooden houses, singing in the hour, making the children cheer.

Moments later, the helicopter touched down on a cobbled street in front of a breathtakingly grand, stony building, the University of Fine Literature. Liesel was almost speechless with joy. "It's as if every stone holds a story," she whispered.

Ferdie was most impressed by his little sister's wistful words, and quickly scribbled them down in his notebook. Nate could feel the stillness of the place, how it seemed to be steeped in history, with a hint of wonderment tingling in the air.

"Can we go exploring?" Harper begged, untying the Scarlet Umbrella.

"Indeed you can." Peter grinned.

Great Aunt Sassy gave Harper a warm hug. "Goodbye, my love," she said. "I must go with the Dutch Opera House

to finish forty-two magenta tutus. I shall miss you terribly, my darling."

"I'll miss you, too," said Harper, giving her a kiss.

"I'll be back in two days to hear all about your adventures." Sassy chuckled, and with a swish of lavender petticoats, she bundled herself back onto the helicopter, waving grandly as it rose into the clouds.

"Leave your suitcases with me," said Brigitte brightly, "and go explore the city. Don't wander too far into the forest, though, and make sure you're back in time for tea."

The children set off into the City of Singing Clocks. The Wild Conductor watched them go, his eyes as bright as those of the birds that surrounded him. "Tell me if you find the mythical Ice Raven," he called, turning to tend to his flock. He longed to follow the four adventure-bound children into the mysterious woods, but he knew if he was to find to the Ice Raven, it was better to wait until nightfall.

Harper, Ferdie, Liesel, and Nate ran hand in hand down tiny winding lanes, breathing in the blossom-sweet scent of the city. Suddenly, Smoke stopped and gave a low growl.

"What's wrong?" asked Ferdie, giving an accidental squeak on the button accordion. You see, wherever the children went, they brought their instruments so they could join in with Harper whenever they liked.

Nate knelt down and listened. There it was. A gentle sighing, as if a few of the clocks were still softly singing.

"I think I know what it is," cried Liesel excitedly. "Some of the clocks are stopped at set times to mark the moments when different fairy tales first began."

The children quickly inspected a little singing clock and, sure enough, written beneath it in tiny silver letters that almost seemed to glow was the word GOLDILOCKS. Everyone smiled at this, and as they moved off through the narrow streets, they couldn't help feeling as if they had stepped into the pages of a story.

Though the city was full of lovely things, soon enough, they all felt the pull of the forest, like a lullaby sung in a voice of black leaves softly calling them closer. Together, they stood on the edge of the ebony trees and peered at the twilight air.

"If anyone gets lost, play three sharp notes," said Harper as the four friends crossed into eerie half-light. "Music is our secret signal."

She followed Midnight along a path that was lined with golden buttercups and beautiful black tulips. She marveled at the size of the toadstools and the way the blue sky was blotted out by dense branches, leaving no space for light. But after a while, she found she was alone. A little girl with a Scarlet Umbrella in a forest of darkening trees.

Chapter Five
INTO THE FOREST OF NIGHT

Liesel was scurrying, scuttling, and skittering like a mouse pursued by an owl. So often had she dreamed of forests full of bears that now she willed them to appear. "Show yourself, beasts!" she bellowed, darting through the trees. But no matter how hard she ran, nothing exciting appeared.

She stopped and kicked a night-colored birch in annoyance. "Of course," she huffed, "I'm being too brave. If I want to be found by something wicked, I'll have to pretend to be lost." And she tiptoed on with delicate toes, gently humming a tune.

She wandered here and she wandered there, picking forget-me-nots, violets, and thistles, until the dark trees parted and Liesel's heart danced high.

Before her stood a cottage made entirely of gingerbread, its door carved from candy canes, its roof dusted with sugarplums, and its chimney crafted from honeycomb.

"A real witch's cottage!" she whispered,

skipping over grass that smelled of peppermint before peering inside. But the windows were misted with icing, and all Liesel could see were strange silhouettes moving around the room.

Silently, she climbed the gingerbread walls, crawled across the sugarplum rooftop, and peered down the honeycombed chimney. The smell of molasses tickled her throat, and she began coughing and spluttering and wobbling dangerously.

Liesel threw her arms wide to catch her balance, but her violin knocked against her toe, pushing her foot into the air. For a moment, she seemed to hover like a bird of prey, and then Liesel found herself falling, lightly as a paper doll,

headfirst into the chimney and down to the darkness below.

You might think that falling into a witch's chimney pot would be frightening. Not for Liesel. So often had she hoped to meet an evil wizard or cruel-hearted grandmother that, as she tumbled softly down, her face was aglow with smiles. Down she fell, down and down, until she landed with a gentle thud on a rocking chair piled with feathery cushions.

Liesel stared around in surprise. She had fallen into a room of the most mysterious folk she had ever seen. Their skin was the color of night and their hair was spun from gold. They weren't witches or wizards—they were something far more special. "Who are you?" Liesel gasped in hushed astonishment.

The eldest of them, a granddad with a long golden beard, glared at Liesel fiercely. "No," he snapped, "who are you?"

Down a dark, twisted pathway, Ferdie was strolling his most serious poet's stroll. It involved long strides and lots of frowning and pausing to think while gazing at the trees. He adored the dark, foreboding woods and the sense of mystery that hung in the air.

As dead leaves crunched beneath his feet, he gave his scarf a serious fling, knocking the pencil from behind his

ear and into a tangle of branches. Ferdie stopped mid-stride in a sort of lunge. All good poets needed a pencil—without it, he was simply a dreamer.

He gave a long sigh and crouched down to find it. As his eyes grew accustomed to the dim light, Ferdie saw something quite wonderful. On each of the black trees, words had been carved into the trunk. Though the bark itself was darker than midnight, the soul of the tree was silver. So the words faintly glowed, as if they'd been etched in fairy dust.

Ferdie leaned closer and found it was a story. He forgot all about his pencil and followed a trail of words: the story of "The Lone Wolf and the Ice Raven."

It was incredible! Ferdie was just getting to a really great part when the bark became too old and faded to read.

He stumbled on, wishing that there were some way of understanding the crumbling words. Then all thoughts of lost words disappeared, for before him was a cottage straight out of one of his mother's storybooks. A cottage made entirely from gingerbread.

He was just in time to see a small, mouse-like figure with a tangle of blonde hair topple headfirst into the chimney. His sister! Ferdie's heart pounded a warning, and he charged toward the cottage door.

63

Chapter Six
A BEAST AMONG THE TREES

A short way from the gingerbread cottage, Nate was moving easily through the midnight woods. So used to darkness was he that the forest at once felt familiar. And yet it was unlike any other place Nate had ever known.

Darkness in the City of Clouds was

always full of sound, but here in the trees there was a rhythm of silence. "It's as if the forest is breathing," Nate murmured to Smoke.

Smoke seemed to hardly hear him. She was different in the forest, too. Her eyes darted like fireflies and her movements became slow and sleek as a hunter's.

A deep and sorrowful growl cut through the dark. The boy and the wolf both froze. Something wild was lurking in the trees.

With a sickening snarl, Smoke leaped, bounding away from Nate like a streak of silver lightning, losing herself in the dark. "Smoke!" called Nate, a tremble

of worry creeping into his voice, but no
reply came.

In all the years they'd been together,
Smoke had never before left Nate's
side. For the first time, Nate felt fearful.
Not frightened of the lightless air or the
strange beast that had growled. Afraid that

his wolf might leave him for a call of the wild woods. "Come back, girl!" he yelled, but all that drifted back was an echo, empty and strange on the breeze. Nate dropped to his knees. How was he ever going to find her?

★

Then there came a thunderclap of howling, as if the forest was being split in half by noise. Nate was sure he heard the snapping of jaws. All at once, Smoke was back beside Nate, nuzzling him gently into a thicket of berry bushes, standing in front of him, shielding him from the other beast. He heaved a huge breath of relief. Smoke hadn't deserted him—she had defended him. As Nate scrambled into the berry bushes, Smoke stood at her full height, her eyes like two burning moons, and howled.

There came another low, sad growl and the plod of heavy paws as the beast among the trees retreated.

Nate threw his arms around his wolf and Smoke's rough tongue licked his cheek. "Come on, girl," he whispered, "let's warn the others about the beast." Together they moved off through the gnarled trees, a pack once again.

In a clearing of black leaves, Harper stepped cautiously forward. She had never been so grateful for Storm, who flitted brightly from tree to tree, and her precious cat Midnight, who galloped back and forth, his white-tipped tail like a candle against the deepening dark.

In the middle of the clearing, Midnight did a most curious thing; he stopped still,

curled up in a sleepy ball, and began to
purr loudly.

"Okay, we can rest here for a while."
Harper smiled, opening up the Scarlet
Umbrella and propping it over Midnight
like a little red tent.

You see, Midnight was a most unusual
cat. Whenever something wondrous was
about to happen, he would always
appear, as if he could pick up the scent
of adventure, or smell magic with his
small pink nose.

Harper perched on top of the umbrella

as if it were a large red toadstool, pulled her piccolo flute out of her pocket, and raised it to her lips, letting the whispers of the forest speak to her. Soon, she was playing a tune of tumbling leaves and midsummer melodies. As the notes wove their way into the wild woods, very slowly the branches above Harper untwined. Fragments of sunlight fell across the clearing, and she caught a glimpse of sky. Harper found herself thinking once again of her dream and the mysterious instrument sewn from silver-lined cloud.

Suddenly, Storm gave a shrill shriek and shot into Harper's hands like an arrow. A dazzling white shape like a

shooting star burned through the trees, singeing the air. It was the wings of a beautiful bird. A bird with feathers paler than ice and a beak made for singing.

"The Ice Raven," Harper whispered, remembering the Wild Conductor's wish to have it lead his orchestra.

At once, she was on her feet, seizing the Scarlet Umbrella and spinning it upside down with Midnight still asleep inside. She leaped in, popped Storm into her pocket, and, with a silent thought, sent the umbrella into the air. But the trees were tightly twisted and Harper had to use every ounce of concentration to steer the umbrella through spindle-like branches without getting stuck.

Two odd yellow lights twinkled at Harper from below, and she gripped Midnight close as a strange, bright-eyed beast emerged from the trees.

Chapter Seven
THE FAIRY-TALE KEEPERS' COTTAGE

"What's wrong, girl?" came a quiet voice. In the thick darkness, Harper wilted with relief. The beast in the trees was Smoke.

"Nate, it's us," she called, lowering the Scarlet Umbrella and holding out her hand.

Nate grabbed it and climbed in, instantly signaling for Harper to hush. "There's something wild in the woods," he whispered.

"What do you mean?" Harper asked.

"Some sort of beast in the trees," Nate explained, clicking his fingers as Smoke bounded up beside him. Midnight awoke and gave a big yawn. As the wolf and the cat snuggled up, Harper suddenly felt hugely thankful that they could fly.

"I think I saw the Ice Raven," she told Nate, "but there's no sign of her now."

Nate gripped Harper's hand. "These woods are strange. I think we'd better get out of here."

Smoke raised her nose and sniffed the

air. The children did the same and caught the far-off scent of gingerbread. "Do you think you can follow it?" asked Nate.

Harper focused her mind on tracing her way through the spiky trees. "I think so," she whispered, trying to keep the umbrella upright and flying in the dark.

For a while, the forest seemed to get denser, and the overlapping branches grew thicker until Harper felt as if they were trapped in a tunnel of never-ending darkness and leaves. She leaned out of the umbrella and used her hands to pull them all from tree to tangled tree until the smell grew stronger and Harper gave a gasp.

"What it is it?" asked Nate.

"You're not going to believe this," she said, smiling, "but I think we've just found Liesel's dream cottage."

Three sharp notes played on a button accordion chimed through the blackness. Harper and Nate turned to each other, and both spoke at the same time: "Ferdie's in trouble!"

With a light *whoosh*, Harper brought the Scarlet Umbrella twirling to the ground. Everyone tumbled out and ran helter-skelter over the peppermint grass up to the candy-cane door, which Ferdie was loudly hammering on.

"What's wrong?" cried Nate.

"The folk in there have got my sister!" replied Ferdie.

"Which folk?" asked Harper, but at that moment the candy-cane door swung open and they came to face-to-face with a man with skin the same rich black color as the trees and a beard so long it touched his toes and seemed to be spun from gold.

Ferdie shook his fist at him. "Give me back my sister!" he yelled.

The old man frowned deeply. "Actually, we've grown quite fond of her," he muttered. "We'd rather like to keep her."

Ferdie went pale. Through the starless dark, Nate reached out and patted his wolf. Smoke gave a rumbling growl.

The man with the golden beard took

a big step back. "Oh, well, it was just an idea," he mumbled. "I suppose you'd all better come in."

The children, the wolf, the cat, and the pink dove found themselves inside the strangest little cottage they had ever seen. On every wall were shelves lined with objects straight out of fairy tales. A red cloak made from the exact same fabric as Harper's umbrella. A spindle, old and delicate and incredibly sharp. Five very ordinary looking beans that seemed to softly sparkle. A slipper of precious glowing glass. And a lock of endless hair.

There, in the middle of the room, her face bright with happiness, sat Liesel, merrily swinging in a rocking chair. "What on earth are you doing?" snapped Ferdie, his sharp German accent much stronger when he was angry.

"Making friends with the fairy-tale keepers." Liesel grinned, gesturing at the family on cushions around the edge of the room.

Ferdie blinked. "The fairy-tale keepers?" he asked.

"Yes," said a tall, willowy woman. "We guard the trees and the fairy tales they hold."

Nate could just make out the silhouettes of a mother and three children, alongside the granddad.

"Each fairy tale is written upon the

trees and has a clock to mark the time it first began," the willowy woman continued. "Only on the eve of the fairy tale's birthday do the characters slip from the pages of their stories and roam the forest."

Harper and her friends stared in surprise. "Y-you mean for one night each year, Red Riding Hood skips through these very woods?" stuttered Ferdie.

"And Cinderella rushes home through these trees?" asked Harper.

"And the three pigs hide from the wolf?" added Nate.

"Yes," cried the littlest fairy-tale keeper, who was so small and smiley she reminded Harper of a pixie.

"The Night Forest is truly amazing," said Liesel dreamily. The fairy-tale keepers nodded proudly.

"I think I found some sort of beast in the trees," said Nate.

"And I thought I saw the Ice Raven," added Harper.

"And I think I found the tale of 'The Lone Wolf and the Ice Raven' written on the trees," Ferdie half yelled.

At this, the mother and the grandfather looked at each other sadly and the three golden-haired children fell silent. Nate felt the air go still and wondered what could be wrong.

"The tale of "The Lone Wolf and the Ice Raven' is the Fairy Tale Unfinished.

The only story without an ending," explained the eldest boy.

"What do you mean?" said Liesel.

"The bark on the trees is too old and crumbly to read," said the middle golden-haired girl, "so the Lone Wolf and the Ice Raven are trapped forever in the forest, until someone discovers how their story finishes."

A sad, low howl, which could only belong to a huge, unhappy wolf, came floating in on the breeze. It was followed by the flapping of dazzling wings. "There they are," said the grandfather, "As real as you or I."

Liesel leaped up and dashed to the window, but before she even reached it, there came on the wind the song of a bird, so sweet and beautiful it could tame the fiercest heart. Everyone stared at one another with wonder. The Ice Raven had started to sing.

Chapter Eight
LONE WOLF AND THE ICE RAVEN

I'm not sure if you have ever heard an Ice Raven sing, but imagine the sound of a thousand hummingbirds learning how to fly, or a nightingale calling to a long-lost moon, and that will be close.

As each of the children listened, they

felt the soft tug of magic and they knew that the Wild Conductor was right— this was a bird whose song could tame Othello Grande's heart and help him win back his place in the Circus of Dreams. Win back the life he so longed for. Win back an adventure of music and clouds.

The children knew they would do anything to help the Wild Conductor succeed, each of them keen to rush back to the University of Fine Literature and tell him the great news. As the bird's song took hold of their hearts, Liesel found it was impossible not to start dancing, so she spun her on toes as lightly as a falling leaf, grabbing the eldest golden-haired boy and swinging him into a polka.

Ferdie felt as if the poetry of the trees had come to life. He at once found a spare pencil and began scribbling a rhyme. For Nate, it was like hearing the whispers of the woods turned into a lullaby, so sweet it could make you weep.

Harper seemed to fall beneath the spell of the song completely. In a dreamy daze, she found herself reaching into the Scarlet Umbrella and pulling out her golden harp. In a streak of claws and fur, Midnight leaped into her arms, knocking the instrument to the ground. The harp clanged loudly, breaking the Ice Raven's spell.

The whole room stared at the black cat with a look of puzzlement. "What's wrong?" whispered Harper, gathering Midnight to her.

"That's a most extraordinary instrument," said the granddad fairy-tale keeper, stooping to pick up the fallen harp and inspecting it. "It is said that with the right song, a harp could draw the Ice Raven out of the trees."

The children nodded, but the fairy-tale keepers looked grave.

"But the Ice Raven must never leave these woods," cried the littlest daughter, "or her story will disappear and she'll never turn back into a maiden!"

Liesel let go of the boy with golden hair, Ferdie stopped scribbling, Nate frowned deeply, and Harper held Midnight tighter, all of them trying not to think of the blue leather-bound songbook, or the man with magpie-feather hair so desperately seeking the mythical bird. "You mean the Ice Raven must stay here forever . . . " Harper murmured, and the family of fairy-tale keepers all nodded.

"Come." The mother smiled. "Let us tell you the tale." And she sank gracefully into the rocking chair, which the children now realized was a storytelling chair. Nate felt around for cushions and handed them out to his friends, then everyone settled down to hear the tale of "The Lone Wolf and Ice Raven."

"Once upon a time, in a deep, dark wood, there was a witch's daughter and a

young prince who were very much in love. They were set to be married by the light of the full moon. But the witch, who was cruel and angry, could not bear to lose the company of her only child. So she turned the girl into a bird with pale feathers and the prince into a huge, hungry wolf. Only at night could they return to their true human forms."

Nate wrapped his arms around his faithful companion, thinking of the growling beast she'd saved him from in the forest.

"By day, the hungry wolf hunts the Ice Raven. By night, the maiden is so afraid of the prince she once loved that she wears a cloak made of moonlight, so bright that

no one can come near her. They have long forgotten who they were to each other and have become enemies."

"How can the spell be broken?" asked Harper.

The granddad sighed heavily. "We don't know," he answered. "The fairy tale was never finished. Its clock was never set."

Liesel leaped to her feet. "What about the witch? Can't she reverse the spell?"

The mother sadly shook her head and continued with the tale.

"When the witch saw how afraid and unhappy her daughter had become, she tried to undo the spell, but alas, she had grown too old and forgetful and died of a

*broken heart, leaving the maiden cloaked in
moonlight and the lonely prince with a cape
of fur to wander the forest forever, becoming
the Ice Raven and the Lone Wolf at the
first light of dawn.*"

A cuckoo popped its little painted
head out of its wooden home and
cooed that it was six o'clock. "You must
head home before night falls," said the
mother gently, "but do come back
tomorrow." Harper tucked the little
golden harp safely inside the Scarlet
Umbrella.

"I will never play it in the forest,"
she promised, hugging the golden-haired
children goodbye.

The eldest took Liesel's hand and

looked at all
of them.
"Come
with me—I know a shortcut."
The four children followed the fairy-
tale keeper boy through a maze of
blackened branches and gnarled trunks
in silence, all of them astounded by the
song of the Ice Raven
and the low howling
of the wolf.
As twigs cracked
beneath their feet and

leaves whispered their secrets, Nate, who knew wolves better than anyone, noticed how incredibly sad the lone wolf sounded. His rough cry was certainly not the growl of a hungry hunting beast, but more of a heartbroken animal, lost and alone. But Nate didn't have time to think about this further, because at that moment they turned a corner and found themselves in the glow of afternoon sunlight.

Harper was amazed to see that the sky over the City of Singing Clocks was a dusky blue; twilight had not even started to fall. They waved farewell to the fairy-tale boy and set off through the winding streets. "How do you think the Wild Conductor will take the news that the

Ice Raven must never leave the forest?" Harper asked nervously.

"Badly," answered Nate.

"But if we explain that she belongs to the Fairy Tale Unfinished, he might understand," suggested Ferdie.

"He'll have to understand," said Liesel. "You can't mess with fairy tales."

Harper smiled, but her feet and her heart felt heavy.

Chapter Nine
A TERRIBLE PLAN

As the first stars began to twinkle, the four children, the wolf, the cat, and the little pink dove reached the University of Fine Literature. It was an incredibly old and majestic building with turrets and spires that seemed to kiss the clouds. Brigitte rushed out to meet them with a basket of warm cinnamon buns. "Come and see your rooms," she cooed, pointing to a set of stairs that led to the university rooftop.

"It's like a garden in the sky," whispered Ferdie as they made their way across a lawn of lavender.

"It's nothing like our rooftop," Liesel told Nate. "There's honeysuckle and lilac and apple trees and even a wishing well in the middle."

Harper smiled as the lavender bristled beneath her feet, the strong scent making her think of her Great Aunt Sassy. It was wonderfully calming after the strangeness of the woods.

In each corner of the rooftop was a

separate turret, complete with a spiral staircase. "Harper and Nate are sharing a turret," explained Brigitte. "Ferdie and Liesel, you're in the turret opposite. Peter and I are in the turret on the far side and the Wild Conductor and his ravens are in the turret over there."

Everyone turned to stare at the turret that was covered by a cloud of dark feathers. The Wild Conductor leaned out of the window and gave a pleasant nod. In the splendor of the sunset, the children couldn't quite bear to tell him the sad news about the Ice Raven. Instead, they sat down to a wonderful picnic dinner of sauerkraut, sausages, rye bread, and apple strudel.

Slowly, the summer moon rose in the sky, and the orchestra of ravens put their fine heads beneath their shadowy wings and slept. The Wild Conductor stared down at the little group on the roof garden and gave a rare, slightly awkward grin. He was in good spirits and was all set for his first journey into the Night Forest. He looked at the blue leather-bound music book and chuckled with glee. At last, the Ice Raven might truly be his. Though, if the legend were true, he would need Harper's help, as the bird could only be summoned by a song on the harp. Still, he might get to see the wondrous bird tonight—he might even hear it sing! He tucked the book grandly inside his long satin coat and made his way toward the picnic.

The view of the City of Singing Clocks was so spectacular that the Wild Conductor paused at the edge of the lavender lawn to take in the sights. Something softly twanged against his foot, and the Wild Conductor spotted Harper's golden harp. "It must have slipped out of the Scarlet Umbrella," he muttered, noticing the umbrella in the corner propped over Midnight and Smoke. Carefully, he picked up the harp to return it, when all at once every cuckoo all over the City of Singing Clocks burst forth to call in eight o'clock, and he was startled into stillness. And in that moment, an idea began to shape in his mind.

Peter appeared at the far end of the roof garden. "Hello," he called to his friends over the chime of a thousand singing cuckoo clocks. He'd had a long day discussing fine literature and was pleased to be back with his children.

Liesel sprang into his arms. "The forest is really magical," she cried.

"There are fairy-tale keepers and a Fairy Tale Unfinished," added Ferdie.

"There's an Ice Raven who can only be drawn out of the forest by a song on the golden harp," said Nate.

"But the Ice Raven must not leave

the Night Forest," Harper said, "or her fairy tale will never be finished."

But the Wild Conductor didn't hear this last part of the story, as he had already slunk into the shadows and vanished into the City of Singing Clocks, clutching the harp firmly.

Chapter Ten
THE MISSING HARP

"I can't find it anywhere!" Harper cried, trying her best not to panic. Liesel dropped to her knees and felt her way through the lavender the same way a little mouse might. Ferdie tightened his serious scarf, but instead of a plan, he came up with a poem called "The Missing Harp."

Peter and Brigitte glanced at each other nervously and started searching quickly around the garden.

Everyone knew how important the harp was. It had been a gift to Harper from her parents, and it was her only way to reach them when she needed to. For you see, Harper's parents lived in the very circus the Wild Conductor dreamed of rejoining. Othello Grande was such a strict ringmaster that the only way Harper's parents could visit their daughter was through the magical harp. When Harper played her dream song, they would drift down on black umbrellas to wherever she was. They simply *had* to find the harp.

Nate and Smoke moved slowly, tracing every step, until they found a harp-shaped dent crushed into the lavender. Smoke put her nose to the ground and gave a pained whine. Nate felt around until his fingers traced the shape of a large footprint. He gave a long sigh. "I think the Wild Conductor may have taken the harp."

Everyone was silent. "Where would he take it?" asked Brigitte, but it was not really a question, for they all knew the answer.

Peter took hold of Harper's shoulders. He had known her all her life, and he looked at her now as fondly as if she were his own daughter. "Go," he cried.

"Get as many as you can in the Scarlet Umbrella and we will follow below by foot."

Harper seized the Scarlet Umbrella, and Midnight leaped onto her head like a little hat. Nate pulled a strand of edentwine from his pocket and attached the umbrella's handle to the wolf's collar. Ferdie grabbed the basket, which was still half full of cinnamon buns, and fastened it to the umbrella with a rope made from twisted tablecloth.

Liesel stared around darkly; there was no room for her and she was trying her best to be calm about it. Nate, who could just make out the small girl glimmering with fury at his side, smiled and took her

hand, his eyes twinkling with a wondrous idea.

Moments later, the City of Singing Clocks was filled with the pounding of unstoppable paws as a wolf the color of stardust tore down the cobbled stones, on her back a small girl with a smile so wild it could have outshined the moon. Liesel was riding on Smoke's back! Floating behind them, shooting past the stars, came the Scarlet Umbrella, towed by the powerful wolf. Deep in the umbrella's dome sat Harper, Midnight, Nate, and Storm; trailing just below in the basket of cinnamon buns rode Ferdie, his scarf billowing in the breeze.

Running after them came Brigitte and Peter, racing as fast as if one of their own

beloved children needed help. "Hurry! Get to the forest—find the harp," they cried.

As the Scarlet Umbrella and the basket of buns approached the dark trees, Harper and Ferdie saw something in the sky that made their hearts shiver. A light was moving, gliding over the black leaves like a drifting star.

"It's the maiden cloaked in moonlight," called Ferdie.

"The witch's daughter!" gasped Harper.

"Where?" asked Nate, but nobody answered, because at that moment Smoke broke into the Night Forest and the children were plunged into darkness. Thin branches pulled at them like wizard fingers, and tree trunks leaned closer together to block out the moon. There was a terrible crunching sound as the Scarlet Umbrella caught in the boughs of an ebony birch. Then the children were tumbling, falling out onto the soft bracken, a sense of unease closing in on them.

Ferdie and the basket of buns got tangled in the lower branches. Nate fell into the undergrowth, his tambourine and pork-pie cap rolling out of reach. Smoke skidded to a halt, hurling Liesel into a mass of berry bushes, while Harper, Midnight, and Storm were flung farther, bouncing from branch to bracken and landing on a bed of glowing mushrooms.

As the children gazed around, they realized they had become separated. Each of them reached for their instruments, only to grasp thin air. In the rush to leave the University of Fine Literature, they had completely forgotten to bring them. They had no way to reach one another; they had no secret signal. And in the deep night of the forest, not even the stars dared to shine. The children were truly alone.

Chapter Eleven
ALONE IN THE DEEP, DARK WOODS

Liesel sat up in the darkness, her heart racing. Slowly, she got to her feet and began to wander through the deep, dark woods, listening for her friends. The forest was quite different by night: bright toadstools glowed like fairy lights, dark-winged moths fluttered, and black hummingbirds hovered in front of indigo irises. A branch snapped behind her and Liesel spun around just in time to see something big and shadowy plodding in the distance. *Perhaps it's Smoke?* she thought, skipping hopefully after it.

It was only when she came to a clearing of dark leaves that Liesel stopped and frowned. This wolf was not growling or prowling or pouncing. This wolf was playing a lute: a very old instrument, like a small guitar. Liesel stepped forward and saw that the wolf was not a wolf at all, but a man in a cape of fur.

"Who on earth are you?" she snapped,

disappointed that he wasn't a wicked beast.

The man turned to look at her and she noticed his big, sad eyes. "By day, I'm a wolf; by night, I'm just lonely," he said.

Liesel gave a light-footed leap of astonishment. "You are the spellbound prince—the Lone Wolf?" she half screamed, at once forgiving him for not being a beast.

The prince nodded. "I am cursed to wander these woods alone, looking for the one I love." He sighed.

"Well, maybe if you stop hunting her when she's an Ice Raven and start acting a bit less wolfish, then things will work much better for you," said Liesel, sitting down next to the prince on a tree stump.

"I'm not hunting her," said the prince in surprise." I'm simply trying to sing and dance for her. You see, we used to sing and dance together under these very trees."

In the pale glow of toadstools, Liesel was silent. So long had she dreamed of being in a fairy tale, and now her moment was here. "Don't worry." She smiled, pulling the prince to his feet. "If she sees you dancing with me, she might just remember who you are."

On the other side of the forest, Harper was pulling a handful of leaves out of her hair. All around her came the soft beat of moth wings and the occasional flutter of a black hummingbird. Even though she was a little afraid, Harper couldn't help noticing the beauty of the Night Forest. She scooped up Midnight and lifted her foot to take a step forward when the world turned bone white. Harper dropped her cat in surprise, peeping between her fingers. Midnight gave a startled meow and huddled behind her ankles.

As the burning brightness lit up the woods, Harper caught sight of a girl in a cloak of dazzling light sweeping through the forest. "The maiden cloaked in moonlight," Harper murmured, tiptoeing after her. Then a terrifyingly tall shadow fell across the maiden's face and Harper froze. It was the shadow of a man upon a bicycle in a long satin coat. It was the shadow of a man playing a small golden harp.

To Harper's horror, the maiden cloaked in moonlight turned toward the harp and stepped into the grasp of the Wild Conductor. Very gently, as if he were handling a precious flower, he lifted the maiden onto the backseat of the bicycle.

"No!" Harper cried, skidding over black moss and slippery leaves as she ran toward them. But the Wild Conductor had already bound the maiden to the bike with edentwine. With a swirl of satin, he climbed onto the front and snapped his fingers. A thousand wide-eyed ravens soared from the trees, lifting the bicycle into the air. "Stop!" Harper screamed, but her voice was lost beneath the beat of black wings.

She fell to her knees, her heart hammering. She had to stop the Wild Conductor before it was too late! Quickly, she plucked the little sleepy pink dove

from her pocket and cried, "Go. Fly. See if you can lead the great birds back into the woods!" Then she turned to Midnight and whispered, "Find the Scarlet Umbrella," and they set off at a run through the Night Forest, Midnight's white-tipped tail like a torch against the dark.

In the depths of the undergrowth, Nate got to his feet. Brambles and branches tickled his skin and ancient bark brushed against him. He whistled softly for his wolf, feeling his way forward, and as he moved, he noticed something quite peculiar.

Carved deeply into the wood of a

tree in front of him were words, very faint and incredibly crumbly, but words to a story nonetheless. Smoke scrambled through the dense woods to her master's side, her rough tongue licking his hands. Nate quickly untied the edentwine and gave her a pat. Then another voice came drifting to their ears, and for a moment, Nate wondered if the forest was haunted—until he recognized the voice.

Alone in the woods
Sat a boy with a scarf,
Stuck in a tree
Tall as a giraffe . . .

It was Ferdie, speaking poetry to the

moon! "Hello," called Nate, hurrying after the sound.

"Nate!" yelled Ferdie, dangling dangerously out of the basket of buns. "I'm trapped in a tangle of tablecloth and edentwine, along with the Scarlet Umbrella."

Nate climbed easily up the tree and wrestled with the basket until Ferdie was sitting beside him on a bough of the ebony birch. Ferdie took a deep, meaningful breath and was just about to continue with his poem, "The Boy of the Wild Woods," when, with a fearsome meow, Midnight sprang into the tree, almost knocking both boys to the ground.

Harper raced to the foot of the tree.

"The Wild Conductor has the moonlit maiden," she cried. "He's taking her out of the forest on his bicycle drawn by ravens."

Nate quickly freed the umbrella and handed it to Harper. "Fly up and see if you can stall him. We'll go and tell the fairy-tale keepers."

In the pitch blackness, Harper smiled. She held the umbrella upright, popped Midnight onto her shoulder, and with a huge amount of concentration, sailed the Scarlet Umbrella up through the twisted trees and into the deep night sky.

Ferdie and Nate scrambled out of the tree and moved off through the woods. Ferdie gazed at the glittering letters on

the tree trunks. In the dark, they shined,
like magical scrolls. "This is the story
of the Ice Raven," he said, recognizing
the tale.

"I know," said Nate. "I can
feel the words."

Ferdie stared at his friend
through the faintly
glittering night.
Then he grabbed
Nate's hand and
tugged him

forward toward the tree where the words became unreadable. "Can you feel what they say?" he asked, his voice a whisper over the beat of his hopeful heart.

Nate gingerly inspected the bark and slowly nodded.

"Then you can solve the Fairy Tale Unfinished!" cried Ferdie. "You can tell us how it ends! You can tell us how to break the witch's spell and free the maiden and the prince!"

Chapter Twelve
SKY-HIGH RESCUE

High above the Night Forest, in the midsummer sky, Harper was flying like never before. Her dark hair streamed behind her and the clouds seemed to roll back as if making way for her. She did not pause for breath until she caught sight of the bicycle towed by an orchestra of ravens. Circling the flock like a dart of pink feathers was Storm, crying out for all she was worth. But the dark birds paid her no attention.

"Hey," called Harper, "you have to stop!"

The Wild Conductor frowned at her and gave a brief shrug. "The Ice Raven can't leave the Night Forest," she yelled. "Or she'll be trapped as a bird forever and her fairy tale will never be finished." But the Wild Conductor waved her away and kept on peddling toward the edge of the trees.

How can I stop him? thought Harper desperately. Ever so softly, her Great Aunt Sassy's voice came drifting from her memory . . .

144

"Music is a magic that soothes the soul."

With a light touch, Harper spun the umbrella upside down and sat down inside it. Deep within its folds was her trusted piccolo flute. It wasn't her harp, but it was the best she could do.

She closed her eyes and began to play with everything she had. The song was fast and fearsome, a frenzy of notes to make your feet dance. Harper was fighting with her flute. Fighting for the Fairy Tale Unfinished—and the harp that was rightfully hers.

At first, nothing happened. Then a single bright-eyed raven turned to watch her, enchanted by her song, and it slowly began to turn in the opposite direction. The other ravens flapped with confusion, and Harper kept playing until her notes touched them. With a swish of powerful wings, every storm-colored bird began wheeling in the sky, turning the bicycle around, and soaring back over the forest, away from the City of Singing Clocks.

The Wild Conductor cried out in rage, but Harper held her nerve and flew the umbrella closer. She paused for a heartbeat to signal to Storm and whisper to Midnight, then she picked up the tune again, playing louder than ever. On the third sharp note, Midnight leaped from her shoulder and Storm swooped from the clouds, both of them landing on the Wild Conductor midair and seizing the golden harp. For a terrifying moment, he began to topple forward. Harper swooped in on the Scarlet Umbrella and caught his arm, pulling him back to balance on the bicycle. Midnight pounced into the umbrella with the harp and Storm fluttered to Harper's shoulder.

The Wild Conductor stared at Harper blankly. "Why are you doing this?" he demanded. "I thought you wanted to help me."

"I do," called Harper, "but not like this. You must return the maiden to the Night Forest."

The Wild Conductor glanced at the beautiful maiden perched behind him and shook his head. He had imagined such great wonders with an Ice Raven to lead his orchestra. He could not give up his dream this easily. He frowned at Harper and quietly said, "No."

Harper bit her lip. There was only one thing she could do. It was a terrible risk, as she had promised the fairy-tale keepers that she wouldn't play her harp in the forest. "Well, this isn't the forest," she whispered bravely, staring around at the clouds, and ever so softly she began to play her harp. This time, it was a song as lovely as a lullaby, gently guiding the ravens back into the lightless trees. The Wild Conductor fretted, but Harper kept on playing.

With a thud of wheels and a swoosh of black feathers, the bicycle landed in a clearing of dark leaves, where a small girl stood beside a man in a cape of fur. The maiden cloaked in moonlight seemed to

suddenly wake up and she gazed at the man in surprise.

"Harper, keep playing!" called Liesel quickly. As notes of beautiful harp music spilled down from the hovering umbrella, Liesel and the prince began to dance. The prince's fur cape swirled around them, so it looked for all the world as if Liesel were dancing with a huge black wolf.

The maiden stared at the dancing prince and suddenly clutched her heart. "Can it really be my prince?" she gasped.

Ferdie and the fairy-tale keepers burst into the clearing, but stopped short when they saw Liesel dancing with a wolf. Ferdie couldn't help smiling—his sister

was dancing with a wild beast! It was one of her wishes come true. At the same moment, Nate and Smoke crept in at the edge of the trees and Nate wrapped his arms tightly around his wolf, just to make sure she wouldn't attack the wolfish stranger. Then he crept over to the maiden and, quietly as a shadow, unbound the edentwine.

Ferdie edged around the clearing to where Nate was crouched. "How does the fairy tale end?" he asked.

"The prince and the maiden have to dance together through the dawn," whispered Nate. "Only then will the spell be broken."

The Wild Conductor, who was

standing close by, suddenly turned quite pale. He finally understood. He stared up at the child floating above the trees in the Scarlet Umbrella. She had been right all along; the maiden and the prince belonged together in their own fairy tale, not his.

The maiden cloaked in moonlight took a tiny step forward. Quick as lightning, Liesel spun the prince across the clearing and darted out of his arms, so he was left instead holding the hands of the maiden. The Wild Conductor pulled the blue leather-bound music book from within his satin coat, and with a heavy sigh he sent it sailing through the air to Harper. The book seemed to open of its own accord, shuffling itself to page ten: "Love's First Dance."

As Harper began to play, the prince and the maiden glided around the clearing, their feet hardly rustling the leaves. "Frederick, is it really you?" the maiden asked.

"Yes, Elvira, it is I!" declared the prince, and they twirled into a moonlit embrace.

They danced and danced, but, as the twinkle of starlight began to grow faint, Harper began to feel tired. Every now and then, her fingers slowed, and so did the dancers' steps.

Ferdie tightened his serious scarf and spoke in his most serious voice. "Grab a partner! We must keep dancing till dawn."

Liesel seized the golden-haired boy's hand and away they swung. Ferdie and Nate danced with both the fairy-tale keeper girls. The Wild Conductor found himself dancing with the fairy-tale keeper mother, while the granddad with the golden beard beat time with his stick. Brigitte and Peter came stumbling into the clearing and instantly joined in with a tango. Storm settled on Harper's head and cooed the tune in her ear, and Midnight meowed, while Smoke happily howled, and the clouds shivered, sending drops of rain falling into the forest in rhythm with the music.

As the first light of dawn spread across the sky, turning the Night Forest the fairest river blue, Harper felt ever so sleepy. Her eyes seemed to be drifting shut, yet somehow her fingers kept playing. And so it was as if from the depths of a dream that she heard a cheer go up and felt Midnight proudly nuzzle her face. She opened her sea-gray eyes and peered over the side of the Scarlet Umbrella to see that the sun had risen over the deep, dark woods and the prince and the witch's daughter were dancing still. No longer creatures of the forest, their fairy tale at long last was almost finished. Then Harper was sound asleep.

Chapter Thirteen
THE MUSICAL CLOUD

When Harper awoke, she found that she was no longer in the Night Forest, but in a bed that wasn't too lumpy or too soft, but utterly, perfectly right. Gathered around her were all of her friends and the family of fairy-tale keepers, all smiling fondly.

"This is for you," said the mother, handing Harper a book. "Thank you for finishing our last fairy tale."

Harper opened the book and gasped. It was the tale of "The Lone Wolf and the Ice Raven." You see, Nate had spent the morning alone in the wild woods with Smoke, carefully feeling for each lost letter on the bark of the ancient trees. Reading with the tips of your fingers is almost like reading with your eyes, but better, because you feel every word in your heart. Once Nate knew the story, he had murmured the words in a soft and secretive voice to Ferdie, who had written them down in indigo ink, and then Liesel stitched the pages of the book

together, pressing them with dark feathers
and fallen leaves from the forest.

Harper turned to the last page of the
book and gave a little glowing laugh.

Then one night a girl with a
harp of gold arrived—a girl
whose rare musical gift could
make the clouds move and the
feet of the maiden and the
prince dance once again. They
spun through the dawn and
the spell was broken, and
they ruled the forest happily
together forevermore.

"You are in an actual fairy tale!" said Liesel with a sigh.

"Yes, but I couldn't have done it without everybody's help," exclaimed Harper.

"There's just one thing left to do," said the grandfather fairy-tale keeper, and he gave Ferdie a cuckoo clock. It was set at five a.m. that very morning. The moment the spell had been broken.

"Could you put it somewhere safe in the city?" he asked. Ferdie blushed with pride. He had never felt so honored.

The children hugged the family of fairy-tale keepers goodbye and set off in a rush for the City of Singing Clocks. Sun glinted off the cobbled stones, and the University of Fine Literature looked quite splendid.

Ferdie and Nate searched the roof garden until they found the perfect home for the cuckoo clock: by the wishing well. Brigitte and Peter put on a grand picnic lunch to celebrate. There was rose lemonade and cherry muffins, bagels, salty pretzels, and thick slices of cheese.

The food was delicious, but Harper wasn't hungry. As she watched the Wild

Conductor slowly releasing his orchestra of ravens back into the wild, she felt the ache of his lost dream tug at her and she crept over to him. "I'm sorry about the Ice Raven," she said gingerly.

"Never mind," the Wild Conductor mumbled as if it didn't matter. But when he turned to face her, his brow was creased with sorrow. "I thought myself the best conductor in the world," he said

in a voice as soft as a teardrop, "but now I see that I am not."

Harper put her arms around him. "But you are," she cried.

"No," he said plainly. "I'll have to find another way to win back my place in the Circus of Dreams."

Harper said nothing, her mind working furiously. Her eyes fixed on a beautiful, bright cloud that was sailing across the city, and all at once, she realized there was one last thing she could try. "Would you mind if I borrowed your bicycle?" she asked.

The man with magpie hair peered at her curiously and nodded.

"Great," Harper said, lifting up Liesel's

abandoned violin and playing three sharp notes.

As afternoon sun swept across the sky turning the river cornflower blue, a girl with dark hair was peddling through the cobbled streets. Her three best friends were balanced on the bicycle, their eyes bright with joy. They wobbled to a stop outside a vintage guitar shop and Ferdie marched inside, reappearing moments later with a length of glistening guitar string. Next, Liesel scuttled into an antique shop and rushed back out clutching a pair of old bellows used to keep fires going. Then, with a silent wish, Harper sent the Scarlet Umbrella soaring into the sky, to scoop up a measure of brilliant white cloud. As

the umbrella floated down, she snapped it shut and popped it into the bicycle's basket. Lastly, Nate and Smoke visited the elegant tailors and came back with a pair of gleaming sharp scissors. With a nod from Harper, they raced back to the University of Fine Literature and piled into Harper's turret.

"Close every window," said Harper breathlessly, and at once her friends did. Then Ferdie blocked the bottom of the door with his serious scarf and Midnight stretched out on top of it to make sure it was secure. Very carefully, Harper opened the Scarlet Umbrella and emptied out the cloud. It was quite spectacular; suddenly, the room was full of mist that coated the children's skin with the quiet wish of rain.

"Here goes nothing," said Liesel in a giddy voice, picking up the scissors and, on the count of three, snipping the cloud open.

A rush of ice and wind poured out, making the children giggle and the wolf yelp. Ferdie delicately pinched one side of the cloud between his fingers, while Nate took the other. Harper raised her harp through the shimmering specks of rain and began to sweetly play.

As her fingers plucked the silken strings, Liesel jumped up and down on the bellows, sending every note of music sailing into the cloud. It was a melody of late-night moons over mystical forests, fierce wolves, and birds with dazzling wings.

"It's the Ice Raven's song," gasped Liesel, and everyone smiled.

Once the last notes had glided into the open cloud, Ferdie and Nate snapped it closed, their fingers trembling against the cloud's iciness. Quick as a mouse, Liesel stitched it back together with the length of glistening guitar string, hardly pausing to blink until it was done. Nate bound the remaining edentwine around the cloud's middle and carefully attached it to the bicycle.

"Let go," said Harper in a tiny voice.

The children all looked at one another

and, at exactly the same moment, they all let go of the bicycle and seized one another's hands. The cloud hovered strangely above them, and the children held their breath as Harper opened the door, hardly daring to look.

Liesel gave a great gasp, Ferdie heaved a sigh of relief, Nate chuckled, and Harper clapped with delight. The instrument sewn from silver-lined cloud—the instrument Harper had long dreamed of—was hovering just above the rooftop. "All it needs now is a rider," she said, smiling, "and I know just the person."

The Wild Conductor stood at the foot of his turret watching the last of his ravens soar away. He pulled his long satin coat tightly around him, and he was just about to go and find Harper and get his bicycle back, when it floated past him. His eyes widened in bemusement as he took in the shimmering cloud above it and saw it was fastened to the bicycle's pedals in such a way that, when you rode it, the cloud would be squeezed in and out like an airborne accordion.

"Climb on," Harper urged, hopping from foot to foot with excitement.

For a moment, the tall man hesitated, then slowly, a little unsteadily, he got on. Everybody waited in perfect stillness, even the wolf, the pink dove, and the cat.

As the Wild Conductor began to pedal, a drop of rain fell from the cloud, and with it came a sound—a little splashed note. As the bike climbed higher and the raindrops fell faster, a rich, beautiful tune came tumbling down, echoing wild wood magic: the tune of a fairy-tale bird played with harp and echoed in rain. It was quite the loveliest sound ever to be heard in the City of Singing Clocks. A song that could tame the fiercest heart.

The best thing about it for Harper was the light that appeared in the Wild Conductor's eyes, a glow of impossible joy. "Follow me," he bellowed, pointing toward the Night Forest.

He didn't need to ask twice. Soon everyone was gathered in the fairy-tale keeper's garden in the middle of the

deep, dark wood, smiling up at the Wild Conductor as he pedaled over the dark tree. The prince and the maiden recognized their song and began to sing in time. The fairy-tale keepers came rushing out, too, and they started up a merry dance while Harper and her friends picked up the tune on their instruments.

From the sky above, the Wild Conductor found himself laughing. He had almost given up on his dream entirely, until a child had shown him it was still possible. A child with a rare musical gift. As the musical rain spilled down on the forest, a plan for a sky-bound concert began filling his mind.

As dusk fell, a curious sound rang through the forest—the whir of spinning blades!

"Great Aunt Sassy!" Harper shrieked, dashing to meet her by the hovering helicopter and falling into her arms.

"Hello, my darling girl," Great Aunt Sassy cooed, wrapping Harper in a lavender-scented embrace. "Have you had a wondrous adventure?" Harper nodded and pointed to the sky, where a dark shape was pedaling through the sunset. "What do you call this fabulous instrument?" Sassy asked.

Harper thought for a moment. "A cloudian," she answered proudly.

"We can make room for it in the

kitchen." Sassy grinned, but Harper shook her head.

"It's a gift for the Wild Conductor," she explained. "One day it will help him win back his place in the Circus of Dreams."

"I'm certain it will," Sassy said, beaming, "but that is an adventure yet to come. For now, my darling, let's celebrate all the wonders of the Night Forest."

And so it was that the girl with the rare musical gift, the poetic boy with the serious scarf, the girl who longed for wicked witches, and the boy with the silver-bright wolf and a knack for finding fairy tales stayed in the Night Forest until the dawn broke once more, dancing with a family of fairy-tale keepers, alongside the prince and the maiden, to magical music that would never be forgotten, music played on an instrument woven from silver-lined cloud.

Much, much later, when all the children had snuggled up in Harper's turret, she tucked her golden harp back inside her Scarlet Umbrella and wrapped her arms around Midnight. Soon they would fly back home to the City of Clouds, but for now, it was time to drift to sleep and dream of dark forests and stories written on trees.

"Good night, Midnight," she whispered, but Midnight was already gently snoring. All Harper could do was join him.

Deep in her dream sleep, Harper rode through a sky of burning stars, her feet pedaling the cloudian. Musical melodies spilled down from the sky, and Harper saw the red-and-gold tent of the Circus of Dreams. Even in her deepest sleep, she knew that the cloudian would help the Wild Conductor win back his place in the floating circus. And she knew that she would help him.